panda series

**PANDA books are for young readers
making their own way
through books.**

O'BRIEN SERIES FOR YOUNG READERS

 panda cubs

O'BRIEN pandas

O'BRIEN panda legends

 flyers

Barry's
New Bed

UNA LEAVY

• Pictures by Moira McNamara •

THE O'BRIEN PRESS
DUBLIN

First published 1999 by The O'Brien Press Ltd,
12 Terenure Road East, Rathgar, Dublin 6, Ireland.
Tel: +353 1 4923333; Fax: +353 1 4922777
E-mail: books@obrien.ie   Website: www.obrien.ie
Reprinted 2000, 2004, 2006, 2014.

ISBN: 978-0-86278-644-1

5 7 9 10 8 6
14 16 18 19 17 15

Typesetting, layout, editing and design: The O'Brien Press Ltd
Printed and bound by Clondalkin Digital Print
The paper used in this book is produced using pulp from
managed forests

The O'Brien Press receives financial assistance from

Can YOU spot the panda
hidden in the story?

When Barry was a small boy
he did not like going to bed.
At bedtime,
he always wanted
to do something else.

'Time for bed, Barry,'
Mum called.
'Let's tidy up.'

'No,' said Barry.
'I have to finish
my jigsaw first.'

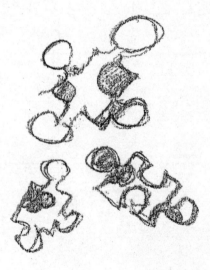

'Supper's ready,' Dad said.
'Milk and chocolate biscuits.
You can have it
when you put on
your pyjamas.'

'No,' said Barry.
'I'm going to play
with Smith.'

Smith the cat had
lots of beds.

In the clothes-basket.

Under the hall stairs.

'I want to sleep in Smith's bed,'
Barry said.

But the clothes-basket
was too small.

Under the stairs was cold
and dark and dusty.

Barry went to his cot.
It was not very big,
but there was plenty of space
for Barry
... and Ted,
... and Frog,
... and Bunny.

Every night Barry said,
'I don't like this cot.
I'm all squashed up.'

Dad laughed.
'When you're bigger,
we'll get you a bed,' he said.

'I'm bigger now,' Barry said.
And one day, he was!

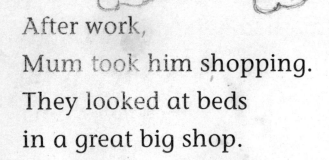

After work,
Mum took him shopping.
They looked at beds
in a great big shop.

Barry hopped on some
when nobody was looking.

At last they chose one.
It was a big, big bed.

Barry was so excited.
At **four o'clock**,
he asked, 'Is it bedtime yet?'
At **five o'clock**,
he put on his pyjamas.

By **six o'clock**,
he could wait no longer.

He skipped upstairs
and hopped into
his big new bed.

It was great.

He loved his soft warm quilt
and his new pillow.

Best of all,
there was lots of space.

When Dad came home,
he went upstairs
to see the new bed.

He read a story
then gave Barry a hug.
'Happy dreams, Barry,' he said.

Mum came and
switched off the light.

'Goodnight, Barry,' she said.
Then everything was still.

Barry looked around the room.
Suddenly the bed
seemed very big
and very empty.

His cot stood in the corner.
Was **something** hiding
over there?

'Mum! Mum!' he called.
'Something's hiding in my cot!'
Mum came in and
switched on the light.

'Look, Barry,' she said.
'There's nothing there,
just your old cot blanket.

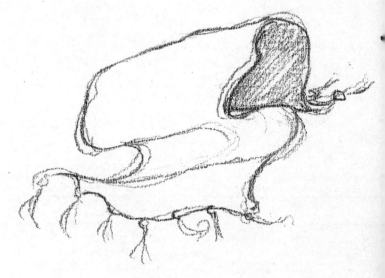

Now go to sleep.'

Barry closed his eyes.
But something lumpy
bumped against his feet.

'Dad! Dad!' he shouted,
'There's a monster in my bed.'

Dad came in.
'Sit up, Barry,' he said,
and he felt
between the sheets.

'There!' he said.
'It's just Ted.
He slipped down
to your feet.
Now go to sleep.'

Barry curled up,
but he still felt strange.
'I'm thirsty!' he yelled,
'I need a drink.'

Mum brought some water.
'Now that's it!' she said.
'I don't want to hear
another word.'

Barry rolled over.
He tried to go to sleep.

Then suddenly he sat up.
'**I can get out of bed myself**,' he said.
'I'll bring Smith up to *my* bed.'

Dad met him at the door.
'Go back to bed, Barry,'
he said.

Barry lay still – for a minute.
Then he thought of his toys.
There was **Winner**,
his little green dog,
and **Goo-goo**,
the furry monkey.

They were
somewhere downstairs.

Off he went to get them.

This was great!

He could climb out of bed
whenever he wanted.

'Oh, Barry!' groaned Mum.
She stayed until
Barry was asleep.
Then she tiptoed
from the room.

Barry didn't wake
until almost midnight.

When he did, it was dark.
The big new bed
seemed huge and empty.
Out he got ...

Mum and Dad's bed was
warm and soft and cosy.
He squeezed in between them
and soon he was asleep.

Next day, Mum said,
'Barry, you're a big boy now,
with a lovely new bed.
Tonight you have to
stay there.
Your toys might get lonely.'

'Okay,' Barry said.

That night,
in Mum and Dad's bed,
there was **Ted**,
... and **Frog**,
... and **Bunny**,
... **Winner**, the green dog,
... **Goo-goo**, the monkey ...

... and **Barry**, of course.

The next night was the same.

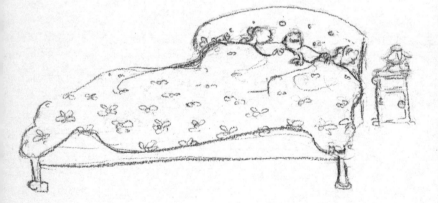

Night after night,
Mum and Dad
were all squashed up
with Barry and his friends.

Mum did her best.
She showed Barry
a robin's nest.

'That's the robin's bed,'
she said.
'She will not sleep
anywhere else.'

Dad showed him the hens
in the hen-house
on their perch.

'They will not sleep
anywhere else,' Dad told him.
'And you must stay
in *your* own bed,' he said.
'Okay,' Barry said.

But nothing changed.
Mum was cross and cranky.

Dad had bags under his eyes.
He put his clothes on inside out.
He forgot to milk the cows.
'I'm *so* tired,' he groaned.

Then one night,
when Barry came in,
Dad jumped out of bed.
'That's it!' he shouted,
and he dashed from the room.

Barry hopped in beside Mum
... with Ted

... and Frog

... and Bunny,

and Winner, the green dog.

But where was **Goo-goo**?

Barry searched everywhere –
in the bed,
on the floor …

He ran back to his room,
and there was Dad,
snoring like thunder,
asleep in Barry's new bed!

A brown furry paw
stuck out behind his shoulder.

'**Goo-goo**!' shouted Barry.

'Wake up, Dad!' he yelled.
'You're sleeping in my bed!'
Dad didn't stir.

'Wake up!
I want Goo-goo.
Get out of my bed!'

He pushed and pulled
and pinched and poked.
But Dad just snored,
and snored, and snored ...

Next morning,
Dad was up early.
He joked with Mum.
He whistled while he shaved.

But Barry was very cross.
'Why did you sleep
in my bed?' he asked.
'I couldn't get Goo-goo
and he was lonely.

Don't sleep in my bed again!'

'Okay!' said Dad.

'You'd better sleep there
yourself.'

So Barry did,

... with Ted

... and Frog

... and Bunny,

... Winner, the green dog,

and Goo-goo, the furry monkey.

They were warm
and snug and comfy.

And so were Mum and Dad!